Cheer Competitions

Impressing the Judges

by Jen Jones

Consultant
Lindsay Evered-Ceilley
Former Denver Broncos Cheerleader and Denver Nuggets Dancer

Director of Business Operations,
Centerstage Starz Theatre and Dance Studio
Centennial, Colorado

Capstone press®
Mankato, Minnesota

Snap Books are published by Capstone Press,
151 Good Counsel Drive, P.O. Box 669, Mankato, Minnesota 56002.
www.capstonepress.com

Cataloging-in-Publication data
  Jones, Jen.
  Cheer competitions: Impressing the judges / by Jen Jones.
  p. cm. — (Snap books. Cheerleading)
  Summary: "Upbeat text provides an in-depth look at the
preparation for, involvement in, and judging of cheerleading
competitions" — Provided by publisher.
  Includes bibliographical references and index.
  ISBN-13: 978-1-4296-1348-4 (hardcover)
  ISBN-10: 1-4296-1348-3 (hardcover)
  1. Cheerleading — Competitions — Juvenile literature.
I. Title. II. Series.
LB3635.J625 2008
791.6'4 — dc22   2007018055

Editorial Credits

Jenny Marks, editor; Kim Brown, designer; Jo Miller, photo researcher

Photo Credits

Alamy/Jeff Greenberg, 19; Richard Wareham, 9

AP Images/Robert E. Klein, 5

Corbis/Bettmann, 6; moodboard, cover; Sygma/Les Stone, 27; Tim Pannell, 13; Trinette Reed, 29

Jamie Christian Photography, 7, 11, 20, 24, 25

Michele Torma Lee, 32

PhotoEdit Inc./Dennis MacDonald, 17

ZUMA Press/Contra Costa Times/Eddie Ledesma, 15; Palm Beach Post/Gary Coronado, 23

1 2 3 4 5 6 13 12 11 10 09 08

Table of Contents

Three Cheers for Competition

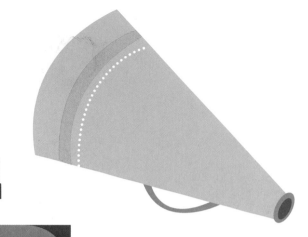

Has cheerleading truly earned a place in the world of sports? The explosive growth of cheer competitions leaves little doubt to the answer. Cheerleaders no longer spend all their time on the sidelines. Thanks to competitions, today's cheer athletes can take center stage.

This book shines the spotlight on the hard-working world of competitive cheerleading. We'll explore the makings of a winning routine, as well as the different types of squads and events. Most importantly, you'll learn how to prepare for competition like a pro. Get ready to reach the top of the cheer crop!

Travel through Time

If you threw a birthday party for the sport of cheerleading, the cake would have more than 100 candles! Cheer has been around since the late 1800s. But it wasn't considered a competitive sport until 1978. That year, CBS aired the Collegiate Cheerleading Championships for the first time.

In the 1800s, Princeton boasted the first pep club, but cheerleading officially started in Minneapolis. University of Minnesota student Johnny Campbell led the legendary yell, "Rah, rah, rah! Ski-U-Mah! Varsity, varsity, Minnesota!"

In the 1980s, cheer became the challenging sport it is today. Teams tried harder stunts, such as cupies and liberties. Gymnastics and snazzy choreography replaced simple pom routines. More competitions popped up, sponsored by organizations like Americheer and Cheerleaders of America.

The popularity of all-star competitions soared in the '90s. All-star teams, created only to compete, ramped up the difficulty of routines. These super teams raised the stunting and tumbling bar to its current level.

In 2000, the fast-paced fun of the movie *Bring It On* showcased two wildly talented squads. The movie proved just how far cheer has come. In cheer, the sky is the limit!

On the Level

Lots of different places and faces make up the competition world. From tiny tots in Nebraska to college grads in New York, almost any squad can compete!

Competitions have categories based on age, skill level, and team makeup (all-girl or co-ed). Teams might also be divided into "ground-bound" and "stunting" categories. In cheer competitions, there is something for everyone!

Events happen at the local, regional, and national levels. On the local level, competitions are held at schools, malls, and festivals. Regional events include state championships and qualifying events for nationals. Nationals are the "big time" competitions. Many teams spend all year preparing for them. The winners become cheer royalty!

Alphabet Soup

Competitive cheerleaders know all the big names: UCA, NCA, USA, and WSF. These companies are hefty forces in the cheer world and host major national events.

UCA: Universal Cheerleaders Association

NCA: National Cheerleaders Association

USA: Universal Spirit Association

WSF: World Spirit Federation

Reaching for All-Stars

Since it began, cheerleading's main purpose has been to root for sports teams. All-star cheerleading has turned that tradition on its head.

Unlike regular squads, all-star teams aren't part of a school. Usually they are housed in special cheer gyms. Their main goal is to rock the house in competition against other all-star squads. Thanks to flashy routines and athletic skills, cheerleading has earned more respect as a sport.

All-star squads compete at six different skill levels. At Level 1, cheerleaders may be very young or just starting out. Only beginner stunts are allowed. Cheerleaders at Levels 5 and 6 are at the top of their game. They perform the toughest stunts and tumbling tricks.

Since 2004, the best of the best have gathered every spring for the Cheerleading Worlds competition in Florida. National competitions sponsor winning teams to go head-to-head for the ultimate title — world champs!

Whatever It Takes

Though cheerleading is tons of fun, hard work happens behind the scenes. Whether school-based or all-star, competition squads demand a lot of time. School squads balance cheering at games and events with preparing for competitions. All-star teams live, breathe, and sleep competition. And let's not forget fund-raisers and team-building retreats!

To take part in competitions, cheerleaders and their families must sacrifice time and money. Many events take place out of town, so traveling is often required. Being a cheerleader takes commitment and dedication.

"To reach cheer glory, you've got to have guts."

Practice Makes Perfect

Most cheer squads practice at least twice a week. They practice after school, at night, or on weekends. In the summer, any time is fair game! When gearing up for competition, even more practice is needed. Good time management skills are a must.

A big part of practice is learning and perfecting routines. Months before a competition, the squad learns a routine's tumbling, dancing, cheering, and stunting parts. After putting the pieces together, the team "cleans" the routine. This means finding the weak spots and cracking down on mistakes. Finally, the polished routine graduates from practice to performance!

Gold Mine

Want to catch the judges' eyes? Sprinkle some high-scoring tricks into your routine.

Full-squad tumbling is sure to impress, especially if everyone can do standing backs or fulls.

Reload from one stunt right into the next. A flashy, fast-paced series of stunts packs on points.

Stand out from the rest. Songs that are all over the radio will probably be in every routine. Get ahead by getting creative and choosing unique music.

Green Machine

In many sports, you have to pay to play. Cheerleading is no different. Competing can be expensive. Cheer team members often pay for uniforms, travel expenses, and competition entry fees. All-stars pay monthly gym fees. School cheerleaders have sports program dues. Add in practice clothes and tumbling or dance classes, and you've got one hefty bill.

Luckily, coaches know cheerleading can be costly. Teams often hold fund-raisers, such as car washes, throughout the season. The money raised covers some or all of the cheerleaders' costs. This lessens the burden on families' wallets and also creates team unity. Now that's worth a million!

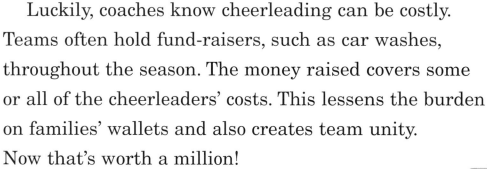

Fun with Fund-raising

Wondering how to rake in the dough? Cash in with these creative ideas:

Pups-n-Poms: Spread some cheer to four-legged friends with a short-term dog-walking business.

Scratch-n-Cash: Hit the fund-raising jackpot with special scratch-off tickets designed for giving, not getting. Players agree to donate up to $5, then scratch the card to find out how much to give.

A Year of Cheer: Make and sell calendars showing off your squad's greatest competition moments.

Teamwork and Trophies

"Together we stand, divided we fall."
In cheer, the old saying holds all too true.
Teamwork is the key to reaching the top.
Competitive cheerleaders must work together
in many ways, from helping each other stretch
out to nailing hard stunts and routines.

Of course, no one expects a group of cheerleaders to get
along all the time. It's normal for competition stress and
friendship drama to cause problems. A squad that knows
how to deal with these troubles shows the mark of a true
team. Respect, communication, and trust are the name
of the game.

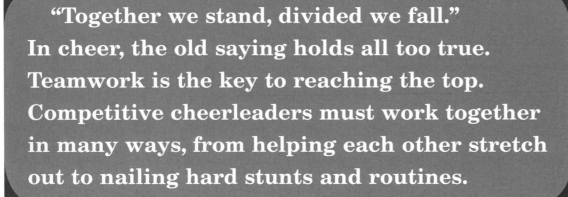

BEST!

"In teammates we trust!"

Taking the Plunge

Team building starts with trust. To build trust on your squad, ask everyone to pick a partner. Blindfold one person in each pair. The blindfolded gal stands directly in front of her partner, facing away. On the count of three, the blindfolded girl falls backward into her partner's arms. Partners should then switch roles and try again. In teammates we trust!

19

Detective Work

Competitions are like snowflakes. Each one is different. Some competitions focus on cheer basics like motions and spirit. Others focus on stunting skills. Before going to a competition, see if you can snag a copy of the scoring sheet. Often, they can be found online or can be requested from the sponsor. You'll be one step ahead of the rest.

Here are some things judges might look for when they watch your routine:

- Sharp, clean, well-timed motions

- Degree of difficulty in stunts, tumbling, and jumps

- Use of signs and cheers to engage the crowd

- Even spacing and use of formations

- Loud, clear voices and spirited facial expressions

- Dance skills and choice of music

- Few mistakes and smooth delivery

- Creative cheers and choreography

As you can see, a winning team must excel in many areas. A well-rounded team wins the trophy!

Just Push Play

A few days before competing, ask someone to record your team during practice. Seeing a video of your routine will help you fix problem areas before the big day.

21

READY, SET, COMPETE!

A Whole New World

Have you ever looked out into a sea of smiles, short skirts, and spirit? If so, you've likely been to a cheer competition. Attending your first competition can be pretty intense. Everywhere you look, squads practice and primp. Music blares, and the excitement is high. Once the competition starts, teams gather to size up their chances of success.

It's a small world in cheerleading, and everyone knows the major players. Just like other sports teams, cheer squads develop rivalries. You're all going for the same award, and all's fair in cheer competition! Of course, teams draw the line at poor sportsmanship. On the flip side, you might also develop friendships with cheerleaders from other teams.

Welcome to Cheer Country

In Kentucky, Texas, and Tennessee, competitive cheerleading is a way of life! These states have traditionally turned out national championship contenders. The competition is fierce in these Southern cheer hotbeds.

Hit the Floor

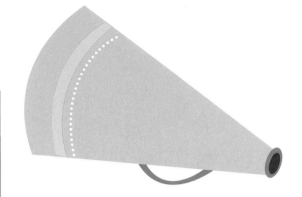

You've heard of celebrities' "15 minutes of fame," right? For cheerleaders, it's 2½! Those precious seconds on the floor seal your squad's competition fate. Even if you've perfected your routine at practice, it's no good if you falter on the floor. There is no denying the pressure of competition.

Many competition routines follow the same basic format. The opening and ending feature dance, stunting, and tumbling set to music. In between is a cheer portion where the squad inspires the crowd to yell along. Though some teams stray from this formula, its winning ways have stood the test of time.

In the end, the team with the most points takes home the trophy. To pump up your point total, follow these trusty tips:

•**Do use signs and cheers geared to rev up the crowd.**

•**Don't step out of bounds.**

•**Do use upbeat, appropriate music.**

•**Don't attempt stunts beyond your skill level.**

•**Do smile and have a great time!**

And the Award Goes to...

Which is more exciting: your squad's big performance or the awards ceremony? It's a tough call. Each has a different kind of pressure. After your time in the spotlight, the outcome is out of your hands. And waiting for the judges' decision can be stressful. Your team will soon find out if the hard work has paid off with a first-place ranking.

For the lucky squads who win, various prizes await. At local and regional competitions, winners might get cash prizes or bids to nationals. National champs get goodies like jackets and incredibly tall trophies. But the best prize isn't one you can touch. It's knowing that you followed your dreams and cheered your way to the very top.

A Winning Outlook

So your squad didn't place first. Maybe you didn't even place. After months of prep, it's easy to feel discouraged when things don't go your way. Is it time to pack up and go back to the sidelines? Of course not! Lots of factors go into winning a competition. Maybe your squad's style didn't gel with the judges' expectations. Maybe another team had more energy or creativity. In any case, it's no reason to give up.

Good sportsmanship is a big part of competitive cheerleading. Losing gracefully and accepting the outcome are signs of a true winner. Sit down with your team to go over the judges' remarks objectively. You'll be able to spin them into gold for your next event — and hopefully take home the gold!

GLOSSARY

bid (BID) — an invitation to attend a higher-level competition

choreography (kor-ee-OG-ruf-fee) — the creation and arrangement of movements that make up cheer and dance routines

formation (for-MAY-shuhn) — the positions in which cheerleaders stand to make a visual shape

ground-bound (GROUND-BOUND) — a cheer team that doesn't build pyramids or throw stunts

qualify (KWAL-uh-fye) — to reach higher stages of competition

rivalry (RYE-val-ree) — a fierce feeling of competition between two teams

sacrifice (SAK-ruh-fisse) — giving up something important for a good reason

FAST FACTS

The University of Kentucky seems to have the magic cheer touch. The team has 15 national UCA titles under their belt, and is the only squad ever to win back-to-back championships twice.

Is there something in the water in Kentucky? Kentucky's Greenup County High School seems to be following in UK's footsteps. The spirited bluegrass team boasts 12 national titles

In 2003, the University of Maryland made cheer history. Their all-girl competition team became the first cheer squad to be declared a varsity sport. Now that's progress.

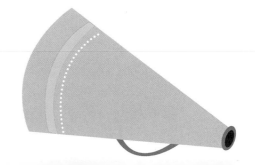

READ MORE

Carrier, Justin, and Donna McKay. *Complete Cheerleading.* Champaign, Ill.: Human Kinetics, 2006.

Jones, Jen. *Cheer Basics: Rules to Cheer By.* Cheerleading. Mankato, Minn.: Capstone Press, 2006.

Wilson, Leslie. *The Ultimate Guide to Cheerleading: For Cheerleaders and Coaches.* New York: Three Rivers Press, 2003.

INTERNET SITES

FactHound offers a safe, fun way to find Internet sites related to this book. All of the sites on FactHound have been researched by our staff.

Here's how

1. Visit *www.facthound.com*

2. Choose your grade level.

3. Type in this book ID **1429613483** for age-appropriate sites. You may also browse subjects by clicking on letters, or by clicking on pictures and words.

4. Click on the **Fetch It** button.

FactHound will fetch the best sites for you!

ABOUT THE AUTHOR

While growing up in Ohio, Jen Jones spent seven years as a cheerleader for her grade school and high school squads. (Not surprisingly, she was voted "Most Spirited" several times by her classmates.) Following high school, she became a coach and spurred several cheer teams to competition victory. For two years, she cheered and choreographed on the cheer squad for the Chicago Lawmen, a semi-professional football team.

As well as teaching occasional dance and cheer workshops, Jen now works in sunny Los Angeles as a freelance writer for publications like *American Cheerleader, Cheer Biz News,* and *Dance Spirit*. She is also a member of the Society of Children's Book Writers and Illustrators.

Index